good deed rain

The Welfare Office © 2019
Allen Frost, Good Deed Rain
Bellingham, Washington
ISBN 978-1-64633-563-3

Writing:
    Allen Frost
Cover Photographs:
    courtesy Michael Paulus
Cover Production: Jen Armitage
    & Aaron "Madison Ave" Gunderson
"The Other Laugh" title page drawing:
    by Rosa Frost
"The Other Laugh" drawings:
    by Allen Frost
Apple: TFK!

"And then I introduce them to Harvey."

—James Stewart

The WELFARE OFFICE

36 Books by Allen Frost

....Ohio Trio....Bowl of Water....
....Another Life,,,,Home Recordings....
........The Mermaid Translation........
..The Selected Correspondence of Kenneth Patchen..
..The Wonderful Stupid Man..Saint Lemonade..
......Playground........Roosevelt......5 Novels......
....The Sylvan Moore Show....Town in a Cloud....
....A Flutter of Birds Passing Through Heaven:
A Tribute to Robert Sund....
......At the Edge of America......
....Lake Erie Submarine....The Book of Ticks....
........I Can Only Imagine........
....The Orphanage of Abandoned Teenagers....
........Different Planet........
..Go with the Flow: A Tribute to Clyde Sanborn..
....Homeless Sutra....The Lake Walker....
....A Hundred Dreams Ago....Almost Animals....
......The Robotic Age......Kennedy......
....Fable....Elbows & Knees: Essays & Plays....
........The Last Paper Stars........
............Walt Amherst is Awake............
......When You Smile You Let in Light......
....Pinocchio in America....Florida....
............Blue Anthem Wailing............
......The Welfare Office......

The WELFARE OFFICE

ALLEN FROST

Good Deed Rain ◊ Bellingham, Washington ◊ 2019

INTRODUCTION

With the exception of "The Other Laugh" and a couple cartoons, these stories were written in just two months. Hot on the heels of *Florida*, this book is in a similar style, but now I was back from vacation, at work in the office again, trying to make sense of it all. In my one brush with fame, *The Bellingham Herald* asked me about my 'day job' and I said it was like working on *The Gong Show*. That's still true, but lately I've been thinking of it as more of a zoo. I'm either a fellow animal, or someone pushing a broom about cages, or both. Either way, this writing is the result.

"Golden Rule"
by Ted Kooser
Acrylic o/c 1978
24" x 24"

3/3

Dear Allen Frost —

Thanks for your letter. I always looked at my insurance job as a means of supporting myself as a poet, and that kept me going through those tedious meetings.

Hang in there —

Ted Kooser

8

Some time ago I read that poet Ted Kooser spent his days in an office too, writing in those early mornings before work. Following that same routine, I wrote to him and he sent me a reassuring postcard. It's important to understand his reply: "I always looked at my insurance job as a means of supporting myself as a poet."

A word about the cover photos my friend Mike Paulus provided. (He's there in the second row). This scene would have been in downtown Seattle c. early 1970s. Just about anyone growing up in Seattle at that time would recognize J.P. Patches, our inspired clown hero. Who better to serve as role model? In fact, I was trying to recreate his TV set here in the office where I work (cardboard clock, cartoons, lots of little wonders with life of their own) before I was advised to take it all down. O, the things that happen here could fill a book, and now they have.

—AF, in the office, July 2019

CONTENTS

Love to Forget
The Failed Artist
The Minnows
10 Minute Birds
The Wrong Path
The Elephant in the Elevator
My Desk is an Apple Tree
Flapping Speed
The Sugar Ants
At Home with a Gorilla
Hamilton the Bird
Circling a Lake
One Simple Mistake
Enjoy Your Time with the Furniture
The 42 Year Old Sandwich
Retired from the Cuckoo Clock
Standing on a Cloud
Over in Memphis

The TWO HORSES

I stopped my bicycle for the traffic light and two horses walked over to talk to me. They saw me sitting in the air on a saddle that wasn't on them. Of course it looked funny and I tried not to listen to their jokes at my expense. Then one of them tossed me a long yellow flower and told me to feed my poor metal horse, it was looking a little thin. Hilarious. Those horses should be booked on *The Tonight Show*. America could use a laugh.

The SEEING-EYE DOG DOG

When I started this job, a woman named Pam worked at the other desk. She was past retirement but she said this was her last year. The same was true for her dog. She needed him there because she was nearly blind. Unfortunately, so was her dog. He was so old he had a seeing-eye dog for himself.

The KANGAROO

A kangaroo took a briefcase out of her pouch. She removed a piece of paper and handed it to me. "I am an accountant and a banker by profession. I work for one of the offshore financial institutions in South Africa."

The LANGUAGE of ANIMALS

These days I'm much more interested in the language of animals. The birds at 4:30, the rabbits whispering under a parked car, a bee bumping into another one coming out of a flower.

300 FEET above TOKYO

On the other side of the book I was reading, someone was chasing a bear. It was young and clumsy and frightened. Then a park ranger (playing a very small role in my dream) yelled, "Don't do that!" and sure enough we all heard the growl of the bear's mother. It sounded loud enough to be a monster 300 feet above Tokyo. I escaped by flying, floating on my back, like lying on a mattress which is how I woke up.

The RABBIT MOTHER

This morning a rabbit walked into the office. I recognized her although she was a lot taller and wore clothes. A blue parka jacket, jeans, tennis shoes. I knew her eyes. She looked exhausted and I knew why. I knew what she had been through and I guessed why she was here. Before she could speak, I said how sorry I was. I found one of her babies dead in the grass. Some creature of darkness killed it and I don't want to say how, but I took care of what was left. "I wish there was more I could do. I wish I could make the yard safer for your family," but how can I? All the way to work I was thinking about it and what kind of world this is. Hidden in the blades of grass are sharp teeth. If only I could stay guard by the nest she left them in. If only that was my job. I would gladly sit beneath the red maple tree until they could care for themselves.

The VOLES

I opened the file cabinet only to find the voles have been at it again. All the folders are in disarray. It will take me hours to rearrange what the voles have done. They have no regard for the alphabet or even for time itself.

A TREE DRIVING a CAR

I don't think it ever tried driving before. It was steering all over the road before it pulled up on the curb, hurried out of the car and ran into the forest. See if you can find that tree when they're all standing still and hiding beneath leaves.

The RETURN of the RABBIT MOTHER

I saw the rabbits' mother again, a day later. I was at the grocery store. Her entire family was dead by then. She seemed to lean on her cart for the strength to move. There was only one thing in it. A radish.

The STOAT
(…a one-minute play…)

A pleased woman sits at a table. Before her is a medium-sized taped up package. She picks up scissors and carefully opens the lid of the cardboard box.

It takes her 10 seconds to cut it open and take out a letter.

It takes 25 seconds for her to read the letter aloud:

"Dear Ms. Bacon,
Thank you for purchasing a stoat. We are quite sure you will be pleased with your acquisition.
We have included one of particular beauty with soft brown fur, gentle face and violet eyes. However, as a word of caution, we would like to offer you some warning.
Stoats are bloodthirsty. Each day they need to eat ten times their body weight. This may cause them to behave in a less than civil manner."

She stops reading and peers in the box, carefully pulling out newspaper wrapping. Nothing in there.

She lifts the box, turns it over and discovers a hole chewed through the bottom.

In horror, she drops the box on the table and leaps onto her chair. She swipes the box off onto floor and crawls onto the tabletop, holding the scissors defensively, staring around herself.

CHECKING *the* MESSAGES

Like any well-intentioned gossip, the telephone holds onto messages that I have to check. Anytime I'm out of the office someone might call. It's almost inevitable. The red light will be flashing to tell me the telephone can't wait, hopping up and down on my desk with another juicy one.

KING TUT'S CAT

That reminds me. When he was a boy he crawled under the house and found an ancient cardboard shoebox. The first thing he thought of was pirates and he hurried to open it. He set the flashlight down so it fanned across the dirt. In a small way, he had been presented with the key to a circus sideshow. For a while that summer all the kids around Elizabeth Park chirped about it like birds. They played and shrieked in the neighborhood at dusk, running from the mummified cat.

HOW DOES IT FEEL?
(...*My rejected* New Yorker *cartoon...*)

"How does it feel to be persona non grata?"

The PAPER AIRPORT

The completion of the paper airport took years and millions of taxpayer dollars. Yes, there was graft and cost overruns and strikes to contend with, but it's finally done. The tower radar spins flimsily and searches for paper airplanes to land. We know people are making them, it's our job to guide them here.

A ROW of WATERMELONS

After all their talk about it in daily meetings, they finally manifested the elephant in the room. I can barely get around it to my desk. It's got one foot firmly lodged in the wastepaper basket. What we need now is a row of watermelons leading out the door to the parking lot. When it gets hungry again it will be somebody else's problem.

The BANK HEIST

An armored car is parked outside. An unemployed hypnotist with nothing to lose stands on the corner holding a newspaper. He's waiting for the guard. He's pretending to read the classifieds.

A SNAIL in a PLAID SHELL

The carpet has not been mowed for weeks and the pile has grown long and furred. A snail in a plaid shell is selling lots. The sound of blades will clack away until it gets cut in rows. When that's done the sprinkler comes on and covers the room with dew.

IT'S BEEN KNOWN to HAPPEN

It wouldn't be right to neglect mentioning the vending machine. It's always standing against the wall. It calls to everyone walking by in the hall. The clink of coins lets you know someone has given in. It's been known to take your money. I've heard people kicking it. Other times, other things fall out. A fortune in a plastic ball. A freshly washed sock. It's been known to happen.

The TIBETAN MONKS

I heard a story about a tour bus full of Tibetan monks stopping at a local fast food restaurant. The sight of all those red robes in line made everyone turn their way. People stopped eating and stared and waited. A woman asked them, "What are you doing here?" The monk who answered her said, "We heard the fries are good."

"There's an old expression…" I told my daughter when we left the garage sale at 307 Shawnee. "It goes: he'd sell the shirt right off his back." The round man with the sunburn watched us leave and she looked at me and said, "Well, it looks like he already did."

The $5 CHICKEN

It's brass and fits in hand like a gold Hollywood award. For a moment I'm Gary Cooper, digging out dollars and coins to match the price written on the masking tape.

RELICS & TREASURES

Who knows what rivers or landfills they lay in: the things that meant the world while they were ours? Don't worry if they're never found. The earth hides treasures and grows them again in new forms

SAND DOLLARS

Last weekend at Clayton Beach a boy came up to me and bragged he was panning for gold in the sand. I've seen those same little flecks glitter in the mud upstream. I told him I'd give him a dollar for every pound he found. He stood there really thinking about it. I left him and then I could hear him in the background telling his parents what I said.

The EGG-TOSSER

Was it the wind or the sun in his eyes? No hope of doing it right makes him drop it every time. Little eggs go airborne like petals twirling everyplace, cracked in the grass with shrieking all around. Dreamworld or real world, he's no good anywhere. Things are fragile in sleep or life and his clumsy attempts are no help at all. His hopes are too big for gentleness, only throwing things away. When it's over, off he goes in soggy footprints, a nursery rhyme failure. He owns no palace or even a big shoe, only a broken barge nailed to the shore. A tattered sail and rigging tied with laundry nobody will steal. He's the egg-tosser, the worst at the game. He can let go but never catch, fumbling with water until the next time makes him try again.

A GHOST STORY *without a* GHOST

On this very spot two years ago someone died. This is not a ghost story though. You won't ever see that custodian haunting the hall. The only ghost is the thought of him that returns every once in a while.

A BIG YELLOW BUTTERFLY

You can tell it's summer. The air above my desk is reeling with swallows and dragonflies. They return every year at this time. A big yellow butterfly rides the ceiling fan carousel. When it drops free, it staggers in space until it finds a wall to hold. It must be dizzy. While it's stuck there like a decal, the fine edges flutter no more than a leaf held underwater.

ALL the SILVER and GOLDFISH

Down in the basement, in the weak light of a single hanging bulb, shadows loom, distance grows like an underwater lagoon and everywhere you look thin filament hangs from the ceiling. Hooks, baited lures, weighted jigs bob and turn like sparks. It was no use. If you were a fish you couldn't resist. A cruel fate awaits them if they bite and up they go, pulled to the rafters.

A BEATLES' SONG

In the broom closet, rolls of paper towels are stored. Pretend they are scrolls. Everything happens according to their script. The directions are simple as a Beatles' song. All you have to do is know that's true and when it happens you can live that way. We are part of something beautiful.

The BEAUTIFUL WORLD

There are reminders of it all around us. You see them happen all the time. The flowers are holding up slow motion signal flags, the bees keep at it day after day, turning the world into honey.

The NEW KANGAROO

Deliveries arrive every day in boxes tall as a giraffe, or flat as a bat, or small as a new kangaroo. I signed for it and the soft yielding cardboard gave a kick. There was a baby inside. I held the weight carefully and checked the package to see who it was addressed to.

The ALLIGATOR'S NIECE

The closest I have to an alligator is the stapler on my desk. There are people who come to me just to ask to borrow it. If they need to remove a staple, I keep the alligator's niece in the drawer. Small teeth sharp as needles.

The OFFICE SPIDER

A tiny spider is making a web in front of my computer screen. Of all things, its web is connected to my cup! What am I going to do? I need my tea! Careful as someone moving invisible beams, I manage to shift that spider's web and anchor it to the telephone. Unfortunately, that seemed to inspire new possibilities for expansion. It's really going gung-ho now, making that web in front of my screen, running back and forth on scaffolding. But let's face it, this office is no supermarket for spiders. How's it going to survive? So I very carefully airlifted the spider to the tree outside. A week later, I got a postcard.

WHEN I'M NOT THERE

When I'm not there, the idea of the office becomes a bird's nest. The kind you find forgotten in a thicket, like a haunted house in the middle of a spine of branches.

Despite a premonition, I have come to this peaceful spot in the woods to write. Is it too quiet? I believe in dreams but only as a separate life on another planet. I'm sitting on moss, surrounded by ferns and young alders. I shouldn't worry. Aren't the birds supposed to warn you if there's danger?

Earlier this morning, I went around the back of a hardware store. I took a look at the loading dock outside the door. An old radio and plastic crates to sit on long enough to smoke a cigarette. I felt like I had been there before. I might have worn one of those blue aprons and worked there. I returned to the parking lot. A friend of mine was calling for his cat. "Wait!" I said, "Is that it?" It was the weirdest looking cat I ever saw. Covered in spots, long shaggy fur like an ice age animal and it was big as a cow. We were lucky we scared it away. So I don't know why I went back looking for it. Dreams follow their own rules of logic. "There it is," I told everyone. It cast a tall shadow on the wall behind the pallet stack. When it appeared it must have been twenty feet long. Someone yelled,

"Run!" and they scattered. I tried but my shoelaces were tied together. I saw the giant cat target me and then it was in the air. I woke up just before it hit me.

I looked at the clock. It was 1:56. I heard a police cruiser go by. I don't think if I fall asleep I'll go back there, I'm sure that version of me is dead as a doornail, but I wasn't ready to take the chance. I got out of bed and went downstairs. I had a sip of water and stopped by the window. I wondered if a big cat was out there. I had a feeling something was watching me. My boss told me a story about living in Montana and I was nervous. It was the middle of the night. A car slid by on 32nd Street and took a sharp right down the dead end. As it turned around, I stepped back behind the curtain. What kind of people are driving around at 2 AM? I tried not to think of that Montana story.

Everything that happens during the day is a clue that takes you somewhere in a dream. I went back upstairs to think about it. The blue light on the alarm clock read 2:03.

What occurred to me was the way

yesterday started. When I was waiting for the 8:30 bus, I saw someone walking towards me in the road. There was something peculiar about him. He carried an aluminum flagpole, wearing a backpack and a soft old fashioned style cap. I said good morning and he greeted me. He had those steely eyes you see in a doomed 1876 cavalry patrol. He was looking for the way to the woods, following the sidewalk like the path beside a concrete stream that ran the edge of the neighborhood. It was only now that I wonder about him, I remember the hat he wore had leopard spots. I took note of that but it didn't seem like an important detail until it returned in the dream, transforming him into some supernatural creature.

So why would I go out to write this in the forest where mountain lions really are seen from time to time. In light of my dream, doesn't it seem like a dangerous place to be? Yes, but this is not a dream. We are in separate worlds even if the shadows fall between us.

RABBIT CRAYONS

Last night we found five new baby rabbits in the corner. As hard as the world is, they are here to try again. They are like the crayon drawings that are taped to refrigerators for a week or so. Sometimes they get lucky and stay longer.

The OLD SHARK

I was sitting in our car watching the traffic across the Wendy's parking lot. I wasn't expecting to have my old boss drive into view. I felt that sudden shock of seeing a shark disturb the water. I had to sink below the windshield, holding the steering wheel like a lifesaver.

The HORSE on ROLLER SKATES

He was strung to the wall like a marionette and once he was free, his feet went every which way. Just for a moment. Actually, we were glad he had roller skates. Once we had him under control, they made moving him much easier. He slid across the bricks on clicking wheels.

LOVE to FORGET

He sees her at the Welfare Agency alone in line, holding a baby.

The FAILED ARTIST

The world gets quieter and the days are only filled by that sound like the tide going out.

The MINNOWS

It takes time because you have to hover your hands over this open filing cabinet drawer and wait for those words to settle like minnows in a shallow sandy pool.

10 MINUTE BIRDS

Sitting on the bench on my 10 minute break, I like to watch the birds. On a sunny day like this, they have the whole world. We're the only ones who need clocks and cars and rooms to sit in.

The WRONG PATH

If I watch the news, I see the opposite of the way it should be. If I listen to the dreary talk around here, I know we're getting further away. So much of what we're doing is taking the wrong path. More plastic crunches underneath and monsters are everywhere along the road and suddenly it's now or never to kick the wheels off the gasoline machine polluting the air.

The ELEPHANT in the ELEVATOR

It's very rare that I take the elevator to the second floor. It's slow and cramped and sounds like a gondola pulled by rusted chains. If someone could convince the elephant to leave, it would probably work better.

MY DESK is an APPLE TREE

Sharing space with the wicker-like weeds, hemlock and nightshade tangles, the old apple tree is overgrown with blackberry vines thick as telephone lines. If you could pick up a phone from the trunk, you would hear 1978 talking. All this overgrowth adds to the taste of the apples that arrive in autumn. By trial and error I have found that a certain amount of jungle helps. In other words, it's the same with the state of my desk.

FLAPPING SPEED

Riding my bicycle home slow enough to give a butterfly a fighting chance to cross the sidewalk in front of me.

The SUGAR ANTS

They're no bigger than a punctuation mark
but if you let them gather into a word or
two, like EAT or STEAL PIE, you'll see
what they can do.

AT HOME with a GORILLA

What started with a gorilla suit has grown. He climbed from the suitcase he was stored in and sat on the couch and watched TV detectives all day, while he cleaned out the refrigerator and cupboards during commercials. By the evening when you returned to your apartment, his long furry feet hung out the open window like canoes and pigeons slept between his toes.

HAMILTON *the* BIRD

Hamilton was walking home from school when he noticed the bird. It ran along just a little in front of him—he was surprised it was so close—and it wasn't scared of him at all, walking along just like him.

When Hamilton stopped, the bird did too. It looked back over its wing and seemed to want to tell him something.

Hamilton remembered the wish he made at school. He was playing with Harper on recess. Everywhere in the cloudy field the dandelions were going to seed and she picked a stalk and said, "I'm going to make a wish!" When she blew, the seeds flew like a hundred little parachutes. She gave him one and said, "Now you."

Hamilton held the slim dandelion stalk and he wished he was a bird. It was what he always wished.

"I bet I know what you wished for," she said. She whispered it in his ear, "You want to be a bird."

"How did you know?"

"The same way I know your favorite song is Old MacDonald's Farm. Only you changed it so all the animals are different birds." She started to sing for him.

That night something bad happened to Hamilton. It happened fast and out of the blue. He died. He didn't feel a thing. And he went to school the next morning because he didn't know.

The same bird was waiting for him on the way.

"Are you ready to be a bird?" it asked.

Hamilton nodded and held his arms outstretched and the next moment he was flying. A hundred birds had taken hold of him and up they flew. They wanted to take him higher, but he told them there was something he had to do.

If you saw him from the ground you would have been surprised to see a boy. The other schoolkids were walking or riding bicycles or arriving by bus and car but nobody noticed him in the air.

He flew around the school until he saw Harper. She was out in the field, the same as yesterday. When he landed on top of the playground fence he laughed and asked her, "What do you think of me now?" But she didn't hear him and she couldn't see him. She was staring at the dandelion in her hands.

"She doesn't know you're here," the bird next to his ear told Hamilton.

"You're invisible," said the bird on his other shoulder.

"But I have to tell her I'm okay!"

"I don't know how you can," answered another bird.

He thought for a moment. He watched her and then he remembered.

This time he did get her attention. She dropped the flower stem. The wish she was working on went wherever wishes go.

She stared at the rows of birds that sang from the fence top. The melody was Old MacDonald's Farm and she knew he was in there singing with them.

CIRCLING a LAKE

She wore her roller skate key on a necklace and liked the way it caught the sunlight in the classroom window. Anytime she wasn't skating she had that reminder. Sometimes I would catch her looking outside and I knew she was out there circling a lake with music playing in her mind.

ONE SIMPLE MISTAKE

I walk past the manhole cover and it's round as a big penny on the bricks. One simple mistake at Olympic Foundry turned the word DRAIN into BRAIN. I stop beside it and listen. I'm picturing the steep ladder down to a dark cement tunnel. Water drips, a stream runs around a goldfish bowl resting on a spindly end table. The globe glows with the light of a pulsing blue brain.

ENJOY YOUR TIME *with the* FURNITURE

"I've been offered work starting as soon as possible at a furniture store in Seattle."

A 42 YEAR OLD SANDWICH

It isn't that hard to turn the corner and find 1977. The years are stacked in layers, like records you can pull down and play. The sunlight is different. For a moment I stare at the place where Woolworths used to be. A song I haven't heard in years and a 42 year old sandwich left on a Formica lunch counter.

RETIRED from the CUCKOO CLOCK

I only hear one bird talking lazily from a tree somewhere behind me. He used to have a job in a cuckoo clock and it took some time before time didn't matter anymore.

STANDING on a CLOUD

They hired a harp player for her retirement party. You can imagine the effect that sound has on someone who spent 20 years working in an office. I told Robert I had to check my pulse to make sure I was still alive. Was I standing on a cloud, with a window to the world below?

OVER in MEMPHIS

1900 miles away from this raining morning, it's also raining. That warm rain over in Memphis is our distant cousin. Years have gone by and the rain on our fir trees only has a black and white photo of them together. Still, you can see the resemblance. There's something in the eyes, something that shines for barbeque and auto parts, the Dollar General, Sam's Discount and it runs in the gutter of Elvis Presley Boulevard.

The WATER on MONDAY

"On Monday, 6/24/19 from 7:00 am to 4:00 pm, the fresh water will be turned off and replaced with salt water. This will affect all water use in the building. As always we appreciate your understanding while this work is performed."

The OLD MOTH

She tottered into the office and told me, "I'm lost." She looked like a cocoon again, with her gray wings wrapped tightly around her. She wore big sunglasses that hid half her face. I took her outside. The morning rain left the grass steaming. I pointed to the building where she wanted to be.

The ZEBRA

A merry-go-round arrived in eleven boxes today. I guess it's my fault I opened one to peek and a zebra got out. It ran around the room in a circle, the only direction it knew, so it was pretty easy to catch and return to the box before anyone was aware.

The FLY TRAVEL AGENCY

Every once in a while, a fly visits the office. This isn't one of their popular tourist destinations. I can imagine the fly travel agency. Brochures and posters feature their dream vacations: a greasy diner, a roadside attraction, or a rodeo. I'm guessing our office is a hard sell. Unless their idea of excitement is circling a room a few times, looking for the way they got in.

INTERMITTENT CHAINSAWS

"On Monday, 7/1/19 from 7:00 am to 4:00 pm, the first floor hallway will be closed due to the removal of trees. In addition there will be chainsaw noise intermittently throughout the day. An alternate route to affected offices should be determined. As always, we appreciate your understanding while this work is performed. Thank you."

WITH a LITTLE LUCK

It's true, all this time I've had a green rabbit's foot in a small gift box beside my telephone. I don't know what else to do with it until that rabbit mother reappeared. I asked her and she said yes, she would take it. She has a brother who ran into lawnmower trouble. The foot looked just his size. With a little luck it will fit.

A RHINOCEROS STAMPEDE

"This is a test of the Office Alert System. In the event of a rhinoceros stampede, get close to the floor where you'll find the freshest air. Try using a phone to let responders know where you are. If the phone doesn't work, then signal from a window by waving a coat and yelling."

A FRIEND UNDERWATER

One summer a long time ago, I had a friend who lived underwater. He had a room like mine set up on the sand. I would take a deep breath and swim down. We would play dinosaurs or cars. He also had a trainset that ran around the seaweed. With my air running out, I would swim for the ceiling. I could hear outboard motors drone like sitars.

The OTHER LAUGH

"Then you will go with me
to my native country. Where
no deaths can claim you,
or tear us apart."

Bela Lugosi
Return of the Vampire
1944

1.

The other laugh was Edward Fenster. He was my partner in a traveling show that took us across the country I don't know how many times. Though not written in the stars, the name of...

...FENSTER & FACK had its day on the metal signs and hand painted boards. I'm still around, I just don't know what to do. I follow the shadow of the same circus life; it's just not the same.

2.

Time has slipped by. Rooms in Saturn Theatre have been rented out. Due to a changing day, they're just trying to make enough to stay afloat. My room is on the corner upstairs. It's the kind of place that is open to the weather.

To be truthful, it's falling apart. I sit by a mended window and watch the street. I listen to music I remember and I like to dream. When I wake, I go to work.

3.

"Hey Charlie!" they say when I sweep past.
"Fack!"
So long moving with a broom, what
can I do? I smile as if the world was a
silver dollar spinning in the stars like a tune.
I sweep around Saturn then I sweep my way
back up the stairs where I began.

Honestly, I never want anyone to feel sad the
way people can. I know enough to pretend.
Even when it's hard, lend your heart to the
day to day anyway. It's been a while and so
the years have left me a character around
here. There are worse things.

4.

I don't know exactly how to describe what has happened to Saturn. Changes have remade it. I take each step slow. I remember well a long time ago.

It only seems gone. The mystery goes on and on. Whatever I daydream is welcome. Whatever I pretend has its place under this roof.

5.

The green wallpaper floats like pond water. In one corner of all this ocean waits the way to my room. Fitted in with the waves on the wall, you have to know where the door hides.

The handle and hinges are disguised and the seams blend with the weeds, but I know where I'm going. I open the door and hear the sound of family.

6.

Before they showed up I must have been alone for years...since Fenster died. Now there is laughter again and drawings of balloon-like creatures on the walls. The night moves them as it breathes into our room.

They are at the window, playing in the carnival of the neon SATURN sign. I feel lighter as I put the broom behind the door and go to them. It's almost like another life waits to begin. It is.

7.

I wish I wasn't so tired from work. I notice
it in my knees and back as I pick the little
girl up. We stand next to the glass. Great
diamonds run down hypnotically.

The peaceful looking aquarium and the
way she looks at everything gives me hope
after such a long day. I know it's a fact she is
learning from every moment, from the colors
of lights, the stories in the street, shadows of
the tree holding its hand up so near to us
and the sounds like strange animal wonders.

8.

Once upon a time in another town, I waited for my friend by a wooden stairway. The steps were made simply out of whatever works. Funny how they seemed to say more about Eddie than words—he used the boards from a bowling alley, split driftwood, an old farmyard fence. Those stairs could have been in a museum.

Some mornings will stay with you, making a painting for remembering. I waited there until he appeared and the picture moved forever.

9.

Walking along the sidewalk, things would happen to us. It's hard to explain. We made up jokes and songs. Our inspiration came from somewhere. It must have been in the air.

Super 8 Films

Talking and laughing as we went along, the towers and the crowded old walls of town were still charcoal, but everything else was our cartoon.

10.

This little girl whose name is Rain wakes me up again. I fell asleep in my chair. She kicks to get down, see more, and play. I set her back on the floor and she has already sprung, running off to the kitchen where her mother Wind is cooking.

I can hear them singing in that yellow folded room around the corner, hidden from view. My chair is turned close to the wooden radio. When the song is right, I feel that flow that changes sidewalks into water.

11.

Music played right into her return. Rain wheeled in like leaves. She ran over to the bookcase and pulled down a picture.

12.

I don't hold much to remind me directly but I have that photograph in a frame. When Rain found it, she held it up to the light and the shadow dropped out.

13.

Seeing old Eddie standing there flat on the wall was such a surprise I couldn't react. Shadows need a light to give them life, but there was no unearthly candle or shine: he was just there, alive.

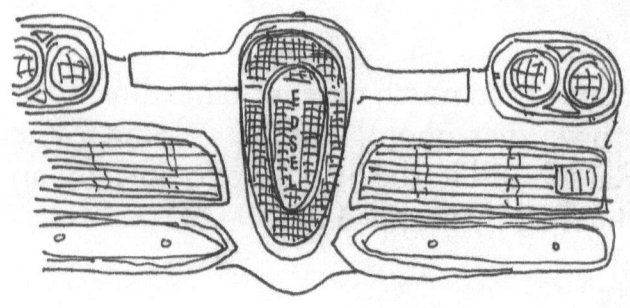

14.

Rain was the one who knew what to do, joking, singing and playing games. I've seen a lot of magic before but nothing in my memory could ever compare.

15.

When Wind called, Rain did a calm thing. She scooped Eddie's shape back into the picture frame and put it where it had been.

Then she ran into the kitchen and left me alone. It took her to tell me what I should have known all along. Next time I want to see my old friend, now I know what to do.

An HOUR with the JABBERWOCK

He walked into the office and looked around and told me he used to work here. With a long sigh, he settled himself into a chair. He told me about the stuffed wolf in the basement, the Mother Goose paintings, and the story of the birds and other things I already forgot. Finally he warned me: you don't want to get an old guy started talking.

A NIGHT in TRANSYLVANIA

The basement storage room was pitch black. This was the sort of darkness that reminds you of a night in Transylvania. He was already scared as he took a few steps inside, felt the rough cold wall to his left, searching for a light switch that wasn't there and he gave up and turned his flashlight on. The yellow beam shined directly on the snarling face of a wolf only a foot away. Half its fur had been chewed off by moths, but its sharp teeth still raised a howl from the catacombs.

LULLABIES OLD *as* EGYPT

The archaeology that comes out of the basement rivals the dynasties of Egypt. For example, the Mother Goose paintings he saved from the dumpster. He brought twenty home and put them on the walls in his barn. They are best seen by moonlight when a row of candles in jam jars leads past the sleeping animal stalls.

The BIRD STORY

The bird story begins with a rich woman who wanted to own every kind of bird. Not to put them in the world's largest aviary on the edge of the bay where steamship passengers would line the deck to listen. She wanted dead birds she could display. Every business in town would get some. Their glassy eyes kept track of everyone. But after she died, all the birds were gone. Nobody could figure out what happened to them, or so they say.

The NIGHTWATCHMAN at the BRONX ZOO

All the stories that aren't written down, the things that happened we will never know. His thermos would rest on top of the locker while he changed out of his uniform at the break of dawn.

The SCARECROW UNION

Before they would let him stand in the cornfield, he had to join the Scarecrow Union. He signed the paperwork, paid his dues and got a good spot along the backroad, half a mile from a silo.

APPLESAUCE

After work last night we stopped at the grocery. The cashier rang up the bag of apples and told us they were her favorite. "Oh," I replied, "they're not for us. They're for our horse." There's no way to take back a joke when it fails—a tart apple can't go back on its branch and wait until it's sure people will approve and the room will fill with applause thick as applesauce.

HORACE the WALRUS

Horace used to work in the employment office. He was notoriously slow and unhelpful. It was a miracle anyone got hired. After he got fired, he got another job at the Gulf gas station on Ellis Street. I found him by accident when I stopped there once. He floated behind the glass of that little booth and gave wrong directions. A year or so after that, they knocked the place out of existence and now all that's left is a plot of gravel.

THEIR HUMBLE BEGINNINGS

Hooligans have hit the office again! They're out on the steps filming each other riding bicycles and skateboards like the stars of a circus. Someone calls the police and they're told to leave. Next year, the video they were making wins an Academy Award. They return and walk around the office with an entourage filming their humble beginnings.

THE PAPER CLIP POND

A Jumbo size box of Item #308-239, holds a
hundred paper clips. If you drop that box it
forms an instant pond. The silver shines like
moonlight.

A GLASS of DOG

The drinking fountain was inspected by the Environmental Health & Safety Office and certified and a sign is glued to the wall next to it: "The water at this tap was tested for lead. Lead concentrations were below the maximum contaminant level. Enjoy drinking here. Fall 2005." Still, there's some doubt that lingers. A lot can happen in 14 years. Our dog is that old and look at her now. If she was our water, held up on four weak aqueduct legs, expect hearing loss, cataracts, and a mind way past learning any more new tricks. How would you like a glass of that?

PIG FARMER BLUES

He raises sixteen pigs every year, feeds them the food from his garden, stands in the middle of them and rubs their backs. It's a good feeling after a long day at the office and summer is a good time to have pigs. Next week he will let them in the turnip field. They're as happy as they will ever be.

The PUPPY TYPEWRITER

The minute I come in the door, it jumps off the desk and runs around my feet, tapping keys and pulling at me. We play chase and tug-of-war with a piece of paper for a while before it finally settles down and takes a nap.

The FATE of the CALIFORNIA POPPY

The California Poppy has fallen over and the smaller flowers hold it up until help can arrive in the form of a pickup, white as an ambulance. A shovel gently lifts it to the back of the truck which is filled with soil warmed by the sun.

A HOUSE ON MARS

119

120

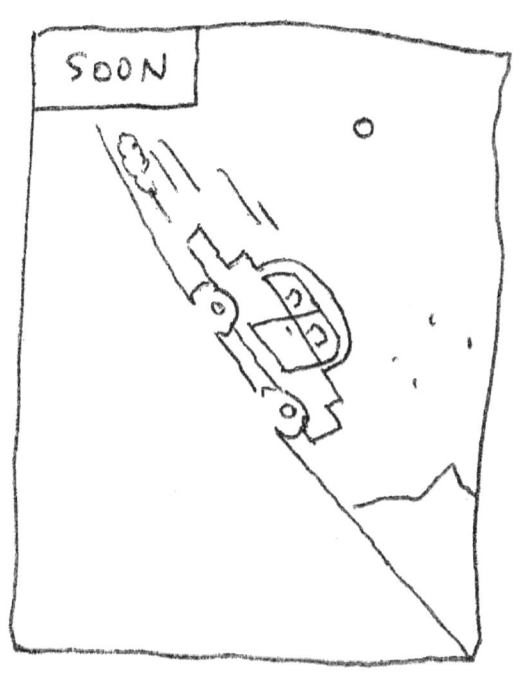

2:30 in the MORNING

Last night my wife woke me up. Actually, it was 2:30 in the morning. She heard something. I listened too and there it went again. A mouse is running back and forth, flying a kite in the attic.

TRIBUTE *to* JACK OAKIE

I was so tempted to call in sick today
and watch a movie. In the kitchen there's
buttered French bread and fresh coffee. It's
raining outside and 1937 Paris is luring me.

A VISIT from RED RIDING HOOD

The birds of the forest follow her and sing with her as she delivers our bin of mail. She told me not to worry. She knows about the wolf. The trees spill down the hill to the edge of the parking lot and something dark shuffles leaves. Sometimes it hides behind parked cars. Sometimes it wears a disguise: even your grandmother's smile might be a little too sharp.

The PENCIL SHARPENER

This morning we have a special guest from Fisher Creek. That's forty minutes by car and not an easy hitchhike. The journey was worth it though. A 50 pound beaver sits on the chair next to me and sharpens pencils. You would think that job was made for it.

The MOTH RESCUE LEAGUE

Rachel loves moths. She caught one in the studio upstairs. She held it under a glass jar on her hand and it tickled her palm. The moth was wearing socks. It left its shoes in the lining of a sweater. O, how it missed the feel of that cotton candy meadow made of wool. When she let it go outside, the moth landed on the pavement. It was raining, its feet were wet. It wondered what happened to that warm sweater.

ANOTHER PIG STORY

They like to root around where there used
to be a barn. It burned down years ago
but they still find nails and doorknobs
and once a rusted key. If only there was a
door somewhere up where there's air and
a lock that needs opening to a room with
everything we ever wanted.

ANOTHER KEY STORY

We rented a house from her one summer when I was nine. She sat on the porch in a long flowered dress and her hair was streaked with white. She waved and smiled to us in the car. I overheard a story about her, how she had her heart broken and she never married but chose to live alone in this house near the ocean and she was happy with that. She gave us a key and we drove down a driveway to the sea. "Watch for the horseshoe crabs!" she called after us. At night they would come crawling ashore and crackle across the rocks.

The PANDA SIGHTING

The morning sound of wet bicycle wheels. Walking in the rain ahead of me is the cat who lives near the office. When it heard the hissing tires, it ran into the woods. It was black and white like a panda and lives that way. Only a few people have seen it, but everyone seems to know the stories.

The CHRONICLE

The deer got into the office last night. They went right along the row of magazines on the shelf and ate every one of them except for *The Chronicle*. I've never seen anyone show any interest in that.

A DAY of PAPER

The reception desk capsized and shipwrecked on the carpet. Broken drawers, an overturned chair, a day of paper, pencils and rubber bands everywhere. A tide pool is left, perfect as the tear of a whale. Little sea anemones grow in it like flowers.

QUITTING TIME

5 o'clock and the bumblebees are heading home, so tired they clip the tops of flowers with their heavy yellow boots.

The WELFARE OFFICE
written by Allen Frost
June-July 2019

POSTCARD from a SPIDER

What's new in the office? Hope everything is good. I'm okay. Just fixed the web for the hundredth time. Was thinking about taking a vacation to see you?

Books by Good Deed Rain

Saint Lemonade, Allen Frost, 2014. Two novels illustrated by the author in the manner of the old Big Little Books.

Playground, Allen Frost, 2014. Poems collected from seven years of chapbooks.

Roosevelt, Allen Frost, 2015. A Pacific Northwest novel set in July, 1942, when a boy and a girl search for a missing elephant. Illustrated throughout by Fred Sodt.

5 Novels, Allen Frost, 2015. Novels written over five years, featuring circus giants, clockwork animals, detectives and time travelers.

The Sylvan Moore Show, Allen Frost, 2015. A short story omnibus of 193 stories written over 30 years.

Town in a Cloud, Allen Frost, 2015. A three part book of poetry, written during the Bellingham rainy seasons of fall, winter, and spring.

A Flutter of Birds Passing Through Heaven: A Tribute to Robert Sund. 2016. Edited by Allen Frost and Paul Piper. The story of a legendary Ish River poet & artist.

At the Edge of America, Allen Frost, 2016. Two novels in one book blend time travel in a mythical poetic America.

Lake Erie Submarine, Allen Frost, 2016. A two week vacation in Ohio inspired these poems, illustrated by the author.

and Light, Paul Piper, 2016. Poetry written over three years. Illustrated with watercolors by Penny Piper.

The Book of Ticks, Allen Frost, 2017. A giant collection of 8 mysterious adventures featuring Phil Ticks. Illustrated throughout by Aaron Gunderson.

I Can Only Imagine, Allen Frost, 2017. Five adventures of love and heartbreak dreamed in an imaginary world. Cover & color illustrations by Annabelle Barrett.

The Orphanage of Abandoned Teenagers, Allen Frost, 2017. A fictional guide for teens and their parents. Illustrated by the author.

In the Valley of Mystic Light: An Oral History of the Skagit Valley Arts Scene, 2017. Edited by Claire Swedberg & Rita Hupy.

Different Planet, Allen Frost, 2017. Four science fiction adventures: reincarnation, robots, talking animals, outer space and clones. Cover & illustrations by Laura Vasyutynska.

Go with the Flow: A Tribute to Clyde Sanborn. 2018. Edited by Allen Frost. The life and art of a timeless river poet.

Homeless Sutra, Allen Frost, 2018. Four stories: Sylvan Moore, a flying monk, a water salesman, and a guardian rabbit.

The Lake Walker, Allen Frost 2018. A little novel set in black and white like one of those old European movies about death and life.

A Hundred Dreams Ago, Allen Frost, 2018. A winter book of poetry and prose. Illustrated by Aaron Gunderson.

Almost Animals, Allen Frost, 2018. A collection of linked stories, thinking about what makes us animals.

The Robotic Age, Allen Frost, 2018. A vaudeville magician and his faithful robot track down ghosts. Illustrated throughout by Aaron Gunderson.

Kennedy, Allen Frost, 2018. This sequel to *Roosevelt* is a coming-of-age fable set during two weeks in 1962 in a mythical Kennedy-land. Illustrated throughout by Fred Sodt.

Fable, Allen Frost, 2018. There's something going on in this country and I can best relate it in fable: the parable of the rabbits, a bedtime story, and the diary of our trip to Ohio.

Elbows & Knees: Essays & Plays, Allen Frost, 2018. A thrilling collection of writing about some of my favorite subjects, from B-movies to Brautigan.

The Last Paper Stars, Allen Frost 2019. A trip back in time to the 20 year old mind of Frankenstein, and two other worlds of the future.

Walt Amherst is Awake, Allen Frost, 2019. The dreamlife of an office worker. Illustrated throughout by Aaron Gunderson.

When You Smile You Let in Light, Allen Frost, 2019. An atomic love story written by a 23 year old.

Pinocchio in America, Allen Frost, 2019. After 82 years buried underground, Pinocchio returns to life behind a car repair shop in America.

Taking Her Sides on Immortality, Robert Huff, 2019. The long awaited poetry collection from a local, nationally renowned master of words.

Florida, Allen Frost, 2019. Three days in Florida turned into a book of sunshine inspired stories.

Blue Anthem Wailing, Allen Frost, 2019. My first novel written in college is an apocalyptic, Old Testament race through American shadows while Amelia Earhart flies overhead.

The Welfare Office, Allen Frost, 2019. The animals go in and out of the office, leaving these stories as footprints.